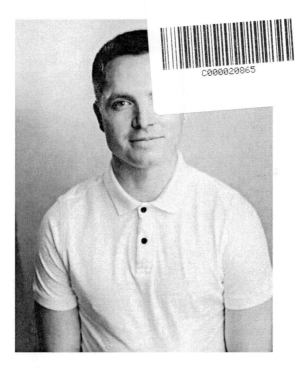

Credit for headshot goes to Nick Corre Photography

Owen Morris is a writer who works professionally as a dancer and teacher. He was born and raised in Cornwall and, at present, resides in London. He trained professionally as a ballet dancer and continues to perform and teach all over the world. Within the UK, he has worked on a feature film, at the Royal Opera House and Royal Albert Hall and in a regional tour, as well as taught throughout London. He danced in ballet companies overseas living in Bulgaria and South Africa and has also performed in Belgium and the Middle East. He lived in Scotland and Devon throughout much of his post-school/student years and lived on the Isles of Scilly for 10 months during the Covid-19 pandemic, where he completed this series of short stories. This is Owen's first published writing.

http://www.owen-morris.com

Owen Morris

SOME PEOPLE COME IN PAIRS
AND OTHER MUSINGS

AUSTIN MACAULEY PUBLISHERS™

LONDON · CAMBRIDGE · NEW YORK · SHARJAH

A CIP catalogue record for this title is available from the British Library.

ISBN 9781398488946 (Paperback)
ISBN 9781398488953 (ePub e-book)

www.austinmacauley.com

First Published 2022
Austin Macauley Publishers Ltd®
1 Canada Square
Canary Wharf
London
E14 5AA

To anyone and everyone who has had an impact on my life however big or small. To fellow book lovers and writers and to people who go fearlessly in pursuit of their dreams.

Some People Come in Pairs

"In this life, we will never truly be apart, for we grew to the same beat of our mother's heart" – Daphine Fandrich

"In case you ever foolishly forget; I am never not thinking of you." Virginia Woolf – Selected Diaries

Prologue

1st September 1939 – the government of the United Kingdom were announcing the evacuation of school children in the cities to rural locations. The children would stay with families from the countryside as a somewhat extended holiday or, as the children saw it, a big adventure.

It was inevitable that all-out war on Germany would be announced shortly. 3rd September 1939, King George VI announces war with Germany. Neville Chamberlain's peace talks had failed, and the world was to enter a bleak 6 years of conflict, tragedy, and bloodshed.

Whilst the city folk of the United Kingdom were preparing for an imminent invasion by the Germans, a family living the furthest south in the UK you could possibly imagine were living a monotonous rural seafaring life. They lived in Cornwall in a village named Sennen Cove just off Lands' End, the southern-most part of the British Isles apart from the Isles of Scilly situated twenty-six miles off the Cornish coast. Beyond Land's End and this small set of islands was New York, 3147 miles away, and the unforgiving formidable force of the Atlantic Ocean soon to be filled with torpedo filled submarines and naval shipwrecks.

The Jago family included a mother, father, four children, one dog named Percy, four chickens and a goat named Penelope. Two weeks prior to the announcement made on the 1st of September 1939 they received an official correspondence from the government asking if they would house twins from London after the imminent threat of attack from Germany.

Jim was a forever patriot of his country having served in World War 1 and didn't even hesitate at the thought of doing their bit for the war effort considering he was unable to serve this time around. This was due to his commitment as a fisherman bringing in vital catches for the supply chain of food and due to a life-threatening injury sustained to his right leg. This was caused by being hit by a landmine when crossing no man's land during a mission. He somehow survived but these injuries would stay with him forever, he would walk with a severe limp for the rest of his life. Mary on the other hand was uncomfortable about two well-to-do children arriving from London. She felt like she had enough to do without having two more mouths to feed.

The parents had been together since they were young and had an unwavering and devoted love for each other. Jim was a fisherman and a volunteer at the Sennen Cove lifeboat station, Mary was a housewife looking after the children, goat and chickens and also worked two days a week in the local post office, which was enough for any busy lady such as herself.

Patrick was nineteen and had rebelled from his father's wish for him to carry on in the family business. He had run away with a lover and moved to Truro where he worked as a postman but as soon as the war was announced, he immediately signed up and was shipped off to fight on the frontline in the army. His lover was slowly a thing of the past. The younger two were Lowenna who was 12 and Lucy who was 10. The fourth child had died in a fishing accident and was Patrick's twin. His name was John and the family had never recovered. Mary would always say that she had four children, they were just all on different timetables and her sons would come home soon.

Saskia & Matthew were twins. They were both 12 years old. The two hated one another. Saskia was the elder of the two by one hour. Matthew had been shy all his life and been bullied by his bullish father on numerous occasions. He had a heart of gold, a charming sensitive nature and a love for nature, books and people. Saskia was a smart, beautiful and confident young girl who excelled in academia and sports. Both had flaxen hair, impeccable soft skin, beautiful green eyes and were below average in height.

Despite their so-called hatred for one another, they were a team, a close-knit unit. They looked out for each other, shared their secrets, and stuck up for each other even when being disciplined by their nanny Betty. Betty was an evil woman they said, she was strict but at heart a gentle caring soul. She had 5 children and her husband worked in a factory making car tyres. They lived in a two-bed flat in Bethnal Green which sometimes had no running water.

The two lived in a London townhouse in Kensington. Their father Charles was a notable MP in the British government and a close confidant of Neville Chamberlain. He was to stay in London and lead the national war effort as an advisor to the war cabinet. When Chamberlain announced his resignation and Churchill began leading the national effort,

Charles was downgraded and went back to his duties as an MP to his constituency of Kensington. He resented his lack of self-importance in leading the war effort.

Charles' wife and mother of the twins, Meredith, was a well-to-do lady who had very little to do with her time. She regarded herself as a full-time mother. That's what she thought anyway but the twins thought differently. She would be with them after supper for around an hour when Betty had gone home for the evening, maybe two hours if she was feeling super maternal. She would talk to them about school, how their father would be coming home late for the fifth night this week and how she hoped Matthew would follow in the footsteps of his father. Bedtime was always too much for Meredith and she sent them on their way at about 9pm every night with not so much as a hug.

Although the twins were beginning to grow up, they were still children at heart and they craved their mother's love. The twins would quarrel before bed and generally would end with Saskia poking Matthew's eyes out but then they would spend hours talking mainly about how Mummy and Daddy didn't love each other and why Mummy was unable to go to the park with them or help them with their homework.

Chapter 1

On 30th August 1939 whilst the children were at school the postman arrived at the door and knocked. "Morning Miss," said the postman. Betty answered the door with her usual abrasive aggressive attitude. "Your employer is to read this correspondence immediately," he said. Betty snatched the letter from him with not so much as a thank you. "Good day miss," smirked the postman as he wandered off. As he disappeared out of view and turned onto the next street he shouted, "war is coming, take care of your family."

That afternoon, Betty spent the day with huge anxiety and irritation. She was desperate to get home and pass on the news to her husband. Meredith turned up later that evening having spent the afternoon having tea with Lady Morgan Smith, the wife of the chancellor. "Afternoon madam, letter for you." The children had been finishing supper when Meredith opened this correspondence. As soon as she had finished the letter Betty shouted from the front corridor "off now madam, see you tomorrow" and slammed the door as she left. Meredith sat dazed and serious in the drawing-room wondering what on earth she would tell her children. The correspondence was informing her that the children were to be shipped off to Cornwall.

"Children," she spoke softly as she entered the playroom. She had spent time contemplating this letter for a while whilst you could hear the children bickering in the playroom. "What is it mother?" asked Saskia curious as ever. Matthew remained quiet and stood half or so meter behind his sister. "You are to go to Cornwall for a while, it is not safe for children in London at the moment." She was dismissive, cold, and clinical in her delivery. "But mother!" spoke Saskia with uncertainty in her tone, her mother quickly interrupted. "I won't have any questions children, that's the end of the matter." There was a short pause like she was thinking about showing her children the love and affection they so desperately needed but then continued. "Betty will help pack your suitcases, now off to bed." The children went off to bed as confused as any young 12-year-old would be.

That evening Meredith waited all evening for Charles to come home and she sat by her piano occasionally playing Chopin sonatas in between periods of silence and tears. Eventually, Charles came home. The children could hear them shouting downstairs. Saskia jumped into Matthew's bed and placed her hands on his ears. "Everything is going to be okay," she whispered.

Chapter 2

Jim had been bringing in the morning catch. The sea was choppy and the sky sombre as if the weather was predicting the mood, the atmosphere of the world and the feeling of war. He was out on his sturdy fishing boat with Lowenna and their dog Percy. Percy loved the water and sat on the bow of the boat on every fishing trip they made, he was a natural water-loving dog. Lowenna had a strong bond with her father, she loved helping him and the feeling of being out at sea. She was petite with long blonde locks and a permanent smiley, happy face. She had dreamed of being a pilot when she was older much to the disbelief of Jim and Mary. The two always supported their children's hopes and dreams and just mentioned that if they wanted to achieve this that they must work very hard. The weather was getting stormier by the minute. It was September, the summer was ending and it had this autumn feeling.

"Come on Lowenna get those nets in before we get swamped by these waves," he said as he began getting ready to row the fishing boat back to shore. Lowenna pulled the remaining nets of lobster from the seabed below.

Lowenna always wondered what mysterious sea creatures lay at the bottom of the ocean. Mary was at home preparing dinner whilst Lucy sat drawing at the kitchen table. "School begins tomorrow and the children from London will arrive." Lucy sat oblivious to what was going on and the huge changes that would begin to uncoil in the world.

That morning of 1st September 1939, the evacuation had arrived. School children from across the cities of the UK, rich and poor, were beginning to be evacuated with their gas masks in check. That morning Betty was preparing her own children for the prospect of evacuation before coming to the twins and helping them. Betty's children were to be shipped off to Yorkshire to stay with their long-lost aunt who had married a sheep farmer. That day, Saskia and Matthew waited anxiously for Betty. Their mother tried to remain positive and as motherly as she could, but she had never had to pack a suitcase before, it was always done for her. When Betty did arrive, there was a strange morbid feeling in the house. Charles had agreed to come home early to see his children off with Meredith. The family would never come together like this.

Betty saw the children off as Charles, Meredith and the twins got into a taxi to drive them to London Paddington station. "Now you be good," said Betty firmly. "Behave yourself, now off you go." "Thank you, Miss Betty," spoke Matthew softly. Saskia just looked at Betty with a strange sullen look, she was probably thinking "thank goodness she is out of our lives for a while." As the taxi drove off, Betty felt a sudden feeling of emotion. She cared for the children deep down and was going to miss them. It seemed the day-to-day worries of her life had hardened her but over the years she grew to really love them as her own.

London Paddington was full of children and parents alike. Trains waiting in earnest to take these children from harm's way. Parents were crying. Children were smiling and wondering what sort of an adventure this would be. Some children refused to let go of their parents' arms. The twins were due to catch the train going the longest way, the 14:07 to Penzance, it would be a six-hour journey. Both twins were equipped each with a suitcase containing a gas mask, a change of underclothes, night clothes, plimsolls, spare stockings & socks, toothbrush, comb, towel, soap, facecloth, handkerchiefs, and a warm coat. A kind elderly lady with a gleaming smile on her face was giving out lunch bags to all children containing a sandwich and chocolate bar.

Shouting station masters were giving information about where which train was going and constantly reminding children not to miss the trains. The family of four walked towards platform 3 just in time to board the 14:07 to Penzance. Meredith held the hands of Saskia and Matthew, probably the most love she had shown them in a long time with Charles closely behind with a glum serious look on his face.

Many people knew Charles as a respected MP and bowed as they passed the family. "Hello, sir," people would say in cockney accents and take off their hats. "Now you be good children," spoke Meredith, "they say you are to write once a month."

"But when will we return?" asked Matthew quietly. "I don't know, son, I don't know," said Meredith helplessly. Matthew looked up at them both, still rather small for his age with an innocent half-broken smile. Charles patted Saskia and Matthew on the head as if to say, "I love you," in the only way he could. Meredith hugged them both, made sure they looked respectable and gave Matthew's collar a good seeing to then sent them on their way. "Off you go now children," she said as they boarded the train.

Meredith and Charles stood closely together not holding hands or linked but somewhat awkwardly trying to look like they were still husband and wife. Charles's father forced him to marry Meredith who was from an aristocratic family in Sussex with lots of money. It was never for the love but for the money and for Meredith's status in society. They waved them off as the train chugged off out of the station. The kids look depressed and worried. As Saskia said the other night, she took Matthew's hand and whispered in his ear "everything is going to be ok."

As the train left London there was a strange sense of uneasiness in the air. One after the other, trains left London with precious children on board as they chugged their way out of the station to various destinations around the Island Nation. London Paddington was full of emotional goodbyes, lots of shouting and noise. As Saskia and Matthew sat comforting each other and the end of the train was out of sight, Charles and Meredith immediately separated in distance and walked out of the station together. There was no talking, comforting or love, just eery silence. Meredith parted in a taxi heading back to the house whilst Charles headed the opposite direction in another taxi. It was back to business for him. There was no eye contact as they parted into their taxis. "See you later dear," spoke Meredith in an uneasy tone. Charles just looked at her and bowed his head in a glum, unemotional way and turned away. When Meredith arrived home, Betty was no longer there and she wept for hours in silence in the drawing-room, realising that reality had hit.

The train flew through the countryside like a cheetah catching its kill. It stopped at a few stops on the way down, but not many. At Bristol, Exeter and Plymouth more children piled in, all heading towards the various destinations with a common thought of adventure, sadness and the unknown. The twins didn't talk much on the way down. Saskia spoke firmly to a child opposite her who might not have been respecting her legroom, but Matthew sat firmly with his eye fixated on his book, his eyes completely dazed and engrossed in the words. He was reading 'The Jungle Book', his favourite book. He had always dreamed of being Mowgli and used to pretend the stair banisters at home were trees he could swing between. "I wonder if where we are going will have trees," he thought to himself.

As the train entered Cornwall over the Royal Albert Bridge which borders Devon, they could see a large sign saying, 'Welcome to Cornwall'. They could tell they were getting close. Three hours later and almost six hours after leaving London, they slowly pulled into Penzance station. The train sounded as tired as the children by this point and needed refuelling like the children who had naively eaten all their food before even reaching Taunton and were starving.

"The last few moments of the train ride were amazing," thought Matthew as, out of the train window, he saw St Michael's Mount, the ocean, seagulls flying over the head and took in the smell of sea air. Sailing boats bobbed up and down on the turquoise ocean, kids ran along the shoreline with kites and dogs ran alongside them with no care in the world. Matthew looked the happiest he had been in a long time,

Saskia on the other hand looked vulnerable and uneasy, quite contrary to her usual self.

By the time the train had arrived in Penzance, the train looked half-empty as most of the children had departed at various other stations in Cornwall. It was very rare for children to be evacuated this far south. The children departed the train with their suitcases in tow and were escorted to the front entrance by a friendly-looking station master. "Welcome to Cornwall my 'andsomes," he half mumbled. He was smoking a pipe and had a sense of calmness in his body language. The station master took the children to a motorcar, waiting for them was an incredibly grumpy looking man who took the suitcases off them and asked them to jump in. It was still early autumn, so it was still light but was beginning to get dark. Both twins smelt the perfume of the sea air, fish and sea salt. The twins were used to London's smog and fumes but nothing like this, they both found it strangely invigorating and refreshing.

The driver drove them to Sennen Cove through the country roads passing fields full of autumn pasture, livestock and bumping into the occasional car or horse and cart. Kids running free in the fields making the most of their freedom before they went back to school and boats on the horizon. Sailing boats, fishing boats and every vessel in between were getting in before the light grew completely dark. Soon it would be too dangerous to go too far out to sea due to the fear of being torpedoed by a German U-boat and being caught up in allied friendly fire. The driver remained silent throughout the whole journey while the twins stared in utter awe out the window. As the car arrived at the front gate of the house in

Sennen Cove, the twins looked at each other as if to say, "We are here."

The cottage in which the family lived in was perched on top of a clifftop overlooking the houses below, it was a small cottage with a porch in the front entrance, a thatched roof and many lobster pots in the front garden. In the garden, there was their goat, Penelope, grazing on the grass. On the other side of the house, there was a back garden with chickens and an accompanying chicken house, a vegetable patch, a wooden swing for the children and a beautiful view of the Atlantic Ocean. Below stood the stunning golden sands of Sennen Cove beach and the small cottages that lay along the shoreline. The house was a steep, sheer ten-minute walk down to the beach and a twenty-minute walk back up, especially if Jim & Lowenna had come in with a huge catch that day. The cottage was small just enough for four people, but the location was idyllic and nothing like the twins had ever seen.

As the car pulled up at the front entrance, four people stood in perfect formation like the bears in Goldilocks and three bears. Jim then Mary followed by Lowenna and Lucy. Percy was pacing up and down sniffing the ground, wagging his tail and barking. "Here we go," spoke the grumpy driver. He spoke as if these children were cargo not humans with emotions and minds of their own. As the twins got out of the car, Percy began barking, wagging his tail and showing them immediate love and devotion. Jim looked at them with a huge gleaming welcoming smile while Mary looked as serious as a strict headmistress and Lowenna and Lucy seemed indifferent in their facial expressions. The girls hadn't been used to people staying here since Patrick, their older brother, ran away a few months ago. Lowenna's eye immediately turned to Matthew with a sense of fondness yet nervousness, Lucy looked at Saskia with her shy but kind, beautiful exterior. Lucy then did the same to Matthew and Lowenna immediately gave Saskia a kind but uneasy half-broken smile.

"Welcome to Sennen," announced Jim in a strong Cornish accent and showed them through the front gate down the pebbled path, "This is Penelope, our goat," said Jim "maybe someday we can teach you how to milk her." There was a short pause "You have also met Percy, our dog, I'm sure. He is alright you know." The kids followed in pursuit with Mary and the girls closely followed behind. As the kids entered the house, there was a sense of uneasiness, like when a lion cub is introduced to its father for the first time. Jim and Mary showed them upstairs to their rooms. The kitchen was small and cramped but had a homely feel to it. There were vegetables laid out on the table, fish to be gutted on the worktop and a hanging decoration by the window made from seashells and corrugated wood. The kitchen led to the living room which had a fireplace, one armchair for Jim, a small second-hand sofa, a spinning wheel and stool and some old toys that the children barely played with anymore. In a small corner at the rear of the living room was a small family photo, including their eldest two sons. Jim led them upstairs. "This is where you will be sleeping Saskia, with Lowenna and Lucy," said Mary from behind, also with a strong Cornish accent but with more sharpness and directness than Jim. There was a bunk bed in which the girls slept and a mattress on the floor. Saskia looked horrified at the thought of sleeping on a mattress on the floor. "This would never happen in London," she thought, closely followed by speaking it aloud. Saskia never could hold her tongue. Matthew just looked at her in disappointment and embarrassment and Lucy did the same. However, Lowenna with a huge smile on her face, she even let a small giggle come out of her mouth. Mary tapped her on the shoulder as if to tell her to stop. "Well maiden, you're not in London anymore, if you're not happy there is the chicken shed in the back garden." Jim looked at Saskia as if to say "Don't worry about her." Matthew was shown to the room next door "this is mine and Jim's room and not to be entered."

"You are to sleep in the living room on the sofa Matthew, I've put you out a rug," said Mary taking Matthew back down the stairs as the girls stayed upstairs and Jim followed in pursuit. "This is where Patrick used to sleep, I expect your rug to be folded every morning before school, I will have no exceptions," she said firmly. "Yes Miss," Matthew softly responded. "Don't worry about her Matthew," laughed Jim ruffling his hair like how his father did but with more kindness and less aggression. Matthew naturally pulled away in reaction. I suppose he was used to this fear back in London. Mary, I think felt guilty for her tone with Matthew as she soon realised that he was innocent and shy but nevertheless carried on with business.

That evening, the family and the new members of the family sat around the homemade dinner table made from pieces from an old shipwreck. The children sat in silence staring at each other throughout the whole dinner, Jim making jokes and asking them questions about London, Mary looking at his husband in disbelief, perhaps even embarrassment at the jokes he was making. Lowenna couldn't take his eyes off Matthew, her young girlish face was fixated on his eyes. Matthew could not always give people eye contact when he felt shy but automatically felt easy looking at Lowenna, he wondered why, he hated girls he thought, his sister is annoying enough.

Immediately after dinner, the children were sent straight to bed. "School starts tomorrow," Mary said, "the girls will walk you to school tomorrow, now off you go to bed." Later that evening, Jim and Mary retreated to their room and Matthew was left downstairs alone with Percy snoring in his basket. He felt alone, scared and deserted. He read his book but was distracted. "Why can't I read?" he thought, "this must be bad." Lucy and Lowenna slept like logs that night. When they were fast asleep, Saskia snuck downstairs to comfort her younger brother. "It's okay Matthew, we will be back in London soon," and wrapped her arm around him. You could hear the calming sounds of the waves crashing on the beach below and a light breeze of wind hitting the thatched roof. Matthew fell asleep in his sister's arms before Saskia returned upstairs. Before leaving, she whispered in his ear and reminded Matthew that they came in a pair. "Matthew, some people come in pairs; I will always be here for you."

The following morning, Matthew was woken very early by the comings and goings, routines, and jobs of the family. Jim was out on the fishing boat by 7am, not to be seen until 6pm that night, and Mary was up cooking porridge and beginning the day's chores. "You will get used to this young man," laughed Mary as she began making porridge with a huge amount of unnecessary noise. That first week of school was hard for Saskia but for once in his life, Matthew felt confident and was looked after by Lowenna. Lowenna, probably fancied him a bit and Lowenna was the popular kind girl in school, so Matthew immediately was liked. Although he barely spoke at all, I think he felt a sense of importance.

He had never felt like this before, he had never been so popular and had never been able to be so confident with one person.

On the other hand, Saskia, the ever-confident bossy young girl, struggled and even felt jealous of her brother. She struggled to make friends, was punished within the first day for answering back a teacher and got in a fight with another girl for copying her work. The teacher could immediately see how bright she was but didn't appreciate her authority being undermined. Lucy was younger than the three of them and played with her friends and looked on at the other three in silence but with complete peace in her mind. Lucy was always the happy, untroublesome child. Even after the tragic death of Patrick's twin brother, Lucy remained relatively brave.

Saskia was told off by Mary so many times she was worried she would give the family a bad name in the village. Whereas Jim laughed it off each time, giving Saskia a wink as if to say "it's alright, I was like you once." Jim found Mary a handful and deeply irritating but loved her with every piece of him, he treated her like a queen, and they were true soulmates. 5 days passed much the same, they hadn't even visited the beach or sea yet. On Thursday night, Jim said "Don't worry, this weekend, the girls will take you down to the beach."

Each night that week Saskia would sneak down and be with his brother and each mealtime Lowenna stared at Matthew in complete admiration. She spied on him from the stair banister once as he sat reading his book. On the 7th of September, Mary arrived home from the post office where she had been working that morning. She came home with a newspaper 'Nazis begin bombing raid in British cities,

17

German U-boat torpedo British Navy vessel off the coast of Scotland.' The blitz had started in London and fighting had started on the high seas of Scotland. The world was well and truly at war.

Chapter 3

The first weekend had arrived and all four children were happy school was out for the weekend. Each mealtime after school, Jim and Mary would discuss all the latest developments and grow deeply concerned about Patrick and the news of where he was being deployed too. Soon the twins would need to write to mother.

On Saturday morning, Jim had gone out early to fetch his catch and Mary was out in the garden fetching eggs from the chickens and hanging out laundry while a fresh sea breeze flew in off the sea. Lowenna had been swinging on the swing waiting for the other three to come out. As all four left out the back-garden exit, straight onto the coastal path, Mary said firmly "Now you be careful, I don't want any trouble." They walked down the rough path to the slipway and onto the beach. Out at sea, you could Jim's boat bobbing in the calm sea and Percy wagging his tail on the stern looking out beyond. They talked – well, mainly Saskia and Lowenna - Lucy and Matthew had a similar silent relationship but kind respect for each other. They hit the beach and began walking along the beautiful stretch of sand.

There were children playing rounders on the beach and the tide was down. Saskia immediately joined in, she was determined to prove herself after a rough week and was immediately accepted as soon as people could see she was a great sportsperson. Lucy joined in as soon as she saw her school friends with them. Lowenna watched on, she was popular and all the boys at school found her attractive. Matthew was acknowledged by everyone but inconspicuously moved up the beach and sat on the sand dunes. He hated sports and sat overlooking the game before getting his book out.

Lowenna immediately clocked this and, after 5 minutes of joining in, walked up the dunes and sat by him.

"Don't you like rounders?" she asked.

"No, I never was much good."

"What are you reading?" she asked curiously.

"The Jungle Book," he responded.

There was a long silence whilst they looked at each other. Whilst they were talking, an RAF fighter jet flew overhead. The whole of Sennen Cove stopped for a while and gazed as the plane flew overhead, Lowenna looked up in total amazement. As it flew into the distance, they resumed conversation.

"I want to be a pilot when I grow up, what do you want to be?" she asked.

"A writer," he responded. Lowenna smiled and said, "I can see that."

"People at school think I like you," she laughed. Matthew looked at her and smiled. There was another long silence and Lowenna moved closer. The two blonde children looked tiny in comparison to the huge stretch of sand the beach was at low tide.

There was a pause in the game down below and Saskia looked up at them, she didn't miss a trick. She always looked out for Matthew, they had an inseparable bond and she always felt responsible for him. "I will take you out on dad's boat sometime if you want." Lowenna looked him directly in the eyes. "I can't swim very well," Matthew was visualising the time he and his family went down to Brighton to their father's second home. He got hit by a wave and got held under for a whole minute. It was highly embarrassing for his father and Charles had mocked him ever since. "It's okay Matthew, you will be safe with me." The pair again looked at each other in silence and Lowenna kissed him on the cheek. A young innocent child-like kiss. Immediately after, Lowenna ran back down the dune and joined in the match, it was her turn to bat, and she scored a rounder hitting the ball hundreds of feet towards the water's edge. Everyone clapped and cheered in admiration. Matthew found a rush of adrenaline flying through his body; a girl had never kissed him on the cheek before. He felt strangely proud of himself and smiled before returning to his book.

The following week at school, the pair became inseparable. Saskia was proving herself to be the smartest girl in the class and, after the game of rounders that weekend, was also becoming very popular - especially with the boys. The teacher, Mrs Clarke, began taking a liking to her and said she wished everyone was as bright as her. The week turned a bit sour for one day when Mary had discovered that the twins were children of the notable Conservative politician Charles Peters. She resented the politicians after losing her brother in World War 1. Jim on the other hand was a patriot and defended the twins' father by saying what a magnificent effort they were doing and how the war would be over by Christmas.

Chapter 4

Halfway through the second week, Saskia began not going downstairs at night to comfort her brother. The dynamic changed, Lowenna would discuss books with Matthew and talk about the stars in the universe and occasionally hold hands. Mary, ever astute, watched from afar as their friendship developed. Jim looked on conscious that his eldest daughter was growing up fast and conscious of how Matthew reminded him of John. At night, he would have regular nightmares about John who, after falling out of the fishing boat, got caught in the fishing nets and drowned as a result. Mary would comfort him, ever the strong character, and stroke his hair to calm him and put him back to sleep. They would fall asleep together in each other's arms.

Each day Jim would limp up and down the coastal path and Mary would watch on wishing she could miraculously make him lose that limp. That second week, each night after they had done their homework and had dinner, they were given permission to play once they had both written letters to their parents back in London. Lowenna and Matthew would sit on the swings and Lucy and Saskia would sit in silence and play games such as tiddly wink and hopscotch on the road outside. Saskia was less homesick now and sometimes used to sneak out after curfew and hang out with the local school children when Mary was upstairs in their bedroom with Jim. Lucy promised to keep it a secret if Saskia helped her with her homework. Many of the local children's fathers had gone off to war and were being raised by their mothers doing similar work to Mary. Mary was lucky Jim was staying.

Lowenna had spoken all week in school about stealing her dad's boat on Friday evening when Lucy, Saskia and her parents were sleeping. Matthew felt uncomfortable about breaking such rules, but Lowenna assured him everything would be fine. She sneaked down at about 11pm and woke Matthew up. "Let's go," she whispered tapping him. "Are you sure this is okay?" he responded quietly. "Trust me," she said firmly. They sneaked out of the cottage and walked down the path holding each other's hands.

Lowenna placed a lantern on the front of the boat as she pushed the boat out to sea, confident as ever. She made sure Matthew was safely inside the boat before jumping in at the last minute and getting her shoes wet. Matthew looked scared and anxious and held onto each side of the boat with extreme grip, he knew if he fell in, he would be toast. All the lobster nets and fishing line were off the boat, and she rowed out a little. As she rowed, she spoke to Matthew before stopping after a good 5 minutes of rowing. "In the photo frame in the living room there are two boys in the picture, who are they?" asked Matthew. Lowenna's energy immediately changed and her facial expression was immediately negative. There was a long pause. "My brothers…" she thought about them as if the world stood still then she continued. "They are my brothers. Patrick is out fighting for our country mum says." Lowenna stopped like she had finished the conversation. "And who is the other?" asked Matthew curiously. "That's John," she said sadly. Tears began falling from her eyes "He died a few years ago in a fishing accident, I miss him every day." Matthew looked sympathetic and shocked and tried to comfort her with his eye contact. "He was mine and Lucy's best friend…" she said "well and Patrick, but he fell out with mum and dad and ran away a few months ago. All I know is he is fighting in a deadly war," she explained. "I feel a sense of responsibility for Lucy but it's hard sometimes." Matthew responded, "I sometimes feel like I'm a burden on my sister," said Matthew softly. "I see how Saskia looks at you when we are together. She loves you; I can tell she doesn't want to lose her twin brother," responded Lowenna kindly.

After a while, she continued rowing some more and then stopped again. "Have you kissed a girl on the lips before?" she asked. "No, have you?" responded Matthew. She shook her head. "Do it now," she instructed. Matthew hesitated for a long time and didn't do anything. "Okay, I will," she said and stood up abruptly and the boat rocked aggressively in the relatively calm water and moved over to Matthew. She moved her soft childlike lips onto Matthew's soft lips, and they touched. She kissed him quickly before moving her lips away. "There we go, did you like it?" Matthew giggled immaturely and nodded with a smile on his face.

After that, Lowenna taught him how to row and they rowed one oar each, oblivious to the ever-stormy feeling in the air and the choppy seas increasing minute by minute. It was eerily dark, and the lantern was the only source of light they had. As they hit one wave it immediately hit the boat with a very unexpected shock and without any warning, Matthew lost his balance and fell overboard.

Lowenna panicked as the waves and strong current immediately separated Matthew from the boat. Matthew could barely swim and was frantically trying to keep himself afloat, gasping for air and with fear in his eyes. "Matthew!" she screamed not knowing what to do holding the lantern visibly to try and locate him in the dark murky waters. She frantically tried to row towards him with all her strength. Shouting and crying she said that she was coming to save him. Second by second Matthew struggled more and more to stay afloat, frantically doing a cross between a doggy paddle and breaststroke but relentlessly getting more tired and more scared. The waves were increasingly getting bigger.

Eventually, she got close enough to him. "Grab this!" she shouted putting out one of the oars she had. Matthew grabbed it exhausted and shell shocked. Lowenna, petite and still a young girl, pulled him in towards the boat. When he was close enough, she grabbed him and with all the strength she could muster pulled him aboard.

"Are you okay?" she cried. Matthew lay on the boat alive but shaken up and silent. "You're safe now," she continued and stroked his forehead. Matthew struggled for air but slowly gained composure, as she stroked his forehead Matthew gasped. "Thank you for saving my life."

She rowed back into the beach as fast as she could, before hauling Matthew out of the boat and onto the shoreline, by this time it was the early hours of the morning and overhead you could hear the Luftwaffe circling over Cornwall lining up to drop bombs on Plymouth. Lowenna was thinking about how she would tell her father what happened after the fatal accident of his brother. Losing Matthew to the elements would be unforgivable, "He isn't even my mum or dad's child," she thought to herself. Telling her mum was not an option she wanted to consider.

In the early hours of the morning, Saskia mysteriously woke up. She never had problems sleeping and immediately knew something was up like she was connected to her twin telepathically. She stood up from her mattress to see the bottom bunk empty as Lucy slept. "Where is Lowenna?" she thought. Careful not to wake anyone, she panicked and she crept downstairs to see the downstairs sofa empty. She panicked again and Percy woke from his basket wanting to follow Saskia as she left the back entrance in the garden and onto the coast path. "Not tonight, Percy," she whispered and closed the door behind him. She hoped she hadn't woken up Jim or Mary.

Saskia had no guide of light but luckily it wasn't too dark. She walked down the path onto the shoreline to see Matthew sitting up straight against the boat on the slipway with Lowenna by his side. She ran towards them, "What's happened?" she said in a panic. "An unexpectedly big wave hit the boat and knocked him off balance and he fell into the sea," Lowenna responded embarrassingly and mortified. "I managed to get him back on the boat before it was too late." "It's okay Saskia, Lowenna didn't do anything wrong we are safe now," he reassured her sister smiling. Saskia hugged him like she was never going to let go. Lowenna took a step back feeling guilty and a bit useless. "Why did I let this happen?" she thought.

"What are we to tell your mother and father?" asked Saskia. "It was my fault," spoke Matthew quietly but Lowenna interrupted. "Nothing!" she said. "We can't, this is our little secret,"

Whilst they were having this conversation Lucy had obviously been woken up and sensed something was up. "Lucy!" said Lowenna surprisingly "What are you doing out of bed?" She was in her night dress and still carried her teddy despite being 10 years old. She had obviously walked down the path by herself not long after Saskia. They explained the situation to Lucy. "This is our secret, okay?", she said firmly "we mustn't tell Mother or Father.". They all agreed and looked at each other. This secret would keep them together. After Matthew had recovered, they walked back up to the cottage. Lowenna and Saskia led the way with the lantern that remained intact despite everything, slowly followed by Matthew and Lucy. "Can I ask you a question?" asked Saskia as they approached the cottage, her voice getting quiet as they approached. "Yes," replied Lowenna. "Do you like my brother?" she quizzed her. "I do," she said uncomfortably. "I always knew, I'm pleased. My brother always needed a friend like you." She said this with a smile on her face and hugged her. The four of them crept back into the cottage, trying to not wake the chickens in the chicken hut or cause Percy to bark, they certainly didn't want to wake up Jim or Mary. In only a few hours, Mary would be up making breakfast and Jim would be in the same boat Lowenna and Matthew had just first kissed in.

Chapter 5

As September ended, autumn well and truly hit. The blitz of cities became more intense by the day. The secret and trauma of Matthew and Lowenna was never spoken, only in private and was not apparent to Jim or Mary. They must have been very good at it as Mary didn't suffer fools lightly. Matthew was shaken up by the whole experience but, with the confidence of the other three, recovered quickly enough.

Jim always hated this time of year, he always knew what was coming and his daily trips out to sea would become shorter, colder and always more dangerous with the change in weather as the sea began to get colder. As the war on the seas became increasingly more volatile the government instructed fishing boats not to go beyond a certain point due to fear of being mistakenly torpedoed. As the days wore on, Saskia became extremely happy with her friends and enjoyed school. In London, they were privately educated and always felt a certain social pressure. Matthew always thought she had a bad attitude before and was extremely arrogant. "This adventure is changing her for the better," he thought. Lucy grew fond of the twins and often would help write Saskia's letters to her mother and father. Saskia never had a great bond with her father. Saskia began playing football with the boys from school much to the disapproval of Mary. There were reports in the local village of a girl playing football. She also began cycling a bike Jim had found in a junkyard when visiting Truro for supplies. She rode it with her friends everywhere and anywhere again to the disapproval of Mary.

Matthew and Lowenna spent every second together. They began reading the same books and walked along the beach day after day. Holding hands, they would run along the water's edge. Matthew always conscious not to go in very far. Sometimes they would fly their kite when the wind was right. They would have conversations about the meaning of life, books Matthew wanted to write and where Lowenna wanted to fly planes to when she was older.

The nights drew in and each report back from London wasn't positive at all. The twins' mother, Meredith, spent her nights in their street's air raid shelters, designed for all the politicians' wives, and spend her days inside the house wallowing away the hours. Charles would stay in the underground shelter at Westminster some nights. Meredith grew withdrawn much of the time and regularly wrote letters to her sister who was married to the Governor out in India. As time went on, the letters from her children became less frequent. She loved her children dearly but often wondered if she was ever really a natural mother after all this time.

One morning after a serious air raid by the Luftwaffe that had bombed a whole street three blocks down from their townhouse, Betty asked if she had heard from the twins. "Any news, madam?" she asked. "They are doing very well at school," she replied. In the time apart from their children, Betty became Meredith's only source of company apart from her time in the air raid shelters at night with other wives of politicians. Although, like the twins, she found Betty irritating, I think she appreciated the company as she spent some days sitting in the drawing-room doing crochet and playing the piano. Some days she used to cry and Betty would come in and comfort her. "It's alright madam, this war will be over soon." Betty's husband had signed up as part of the 'Forgotten Army' leading the war effort down the mines, this was after the factory he worked in was bombed. Betty never really felt so much alone as Meredith, despite her children living with her long-lost aunt and her husband away, she belonged to a community in East London and her social class meant there was no competition or hierarchy.

One weekend, the four children were given permission to board the bus to the nearest local town, Penzance, for the day. For Saskia's birthday in October, their mother sent down them a shilling each. Going into a town was a huge occasion for the twins, but for Lowenna and Lucy it felt like normal. They went into town and went into the local sweet shop and played with local children in the streets. The streets were quiet, with few men in sight. They returned later in the day and walked to Lands' End about a half an hour's walk from Sennen Cove. It really was the end of the UK. Beyond this point were a few isolated rocks and the lighthouse that flashed at night, sounding its horn when it was misty. Beyond that was the desolate ocean and the Isles of Scilly.

"One day, I want to fly to New York", said Lowenna. "What do you want to do Saskia?" she continued. "I want to cycle the length and breadth of the country and become a lawyer," replied Saskia. "If you go that way, what's the furthest north?" asked Matthew pointing northward. "John O'Groats," said Saskia with confidence, "in Scotland, I want to cycle there one day." Lucy spoke before being asked "I'm going to be a painter," she said proudly and before Matthew could speak. Lowenna said proudly "And you, Matthew, will be the new Rudyard Kipling." The four stood at what felt like the end of the earth, the rain started and the wind came in off the ocean. "We must be getting back," said Lowenna and they walked down the winding coast path back to the cottage where Mary had prepared toad in the hole while Jim was resting. That month would be one of the most ruthless attacks on British cities by the Nazis. Christmas came round in a flash. The prospect for the twins was they were to stay in Cornwall over Christmas. Meredith wrote a letter to them two weeks before Christmas saying:

Dear my young ones,

Me and your father are no longer together. I am to go to India this Christmas and visit your Aunt Julie I may stay longer if necessary. Dear Betty died not long ago. You will stay with the Jago Family this Christmas. I will send you gifts. Be good now children.

Mother

What the letter didn't say was Charles had been having a long-term affair with a secretary of Winston Churchill and had somehow found himself back in a position of power in Churchill's cabinet working as the Secretary of Labour and Agriculture. The day he left was a Friday after the new announcement of his position. To be honest Meredith wasn't surprised but nevertheless heartbroken. Outside lay all her suitcases packed by Betty the day before she died.

Betty had been with Meredith all evening comforting her and was hit in an air raid as she was rushing home and trying and take cover in one of the underground stations used as an air raid shelter. Charles had fired Betty that day when it was announced Meredith would be moving out. Meredith felt a desperate sense of guilt about the whole situation. Charles felt nothing and the new secretary moved in with him the next day.

When the letter arrived, they had been at school, but Mary had read in the papers that their father would be reinstated as secretary for labour and agriculture. The twins read this letter together. They both cried with unstoppable emotion. Saskia tried to see a different perspective. "They never did love each other, Mother and Father will soon become happier without each other. I'm sorry for Betty, she never was a bad person. I do hope her children and husband are okay. I wish I had said goodbye to her properly." Matthew was beside himself in obvious distress. They squeezed each other tightly processing all that had happened. Jim was out and Mary was delivering chicken eggs to the local shopkeeper. Lucy and Lowenna came downstairs a while later, aware the twins needed time to themselves. Matthew continued to weep but Saskia composed herself to explain everything that had happened. Lucy hugged her first and then Matthew before embracing in a group hug. Lowenna watched from afar processing it all before coming in and joining them. "It's okay, your part of our family now," she said with sympathy. Not long later, Mary returned home to see the 4 children sat outside the cottage by the coast path overlooking the cliff edge. It was cold and almost dark despite only being 4pm, they were wrapped up warm and embracing each other. Mary watched them from the kitchen window. It reminded her of when all four of her children were together – and how much she missed her boys. That evening, Saskia explained what had happened and Mary, for the first time, showed her sensitive side and hugged them both. Jim returned a little while later and immediately embraced them both. That night, Saskia and Matthew fell asleep by each other's side. Lowenna so wanted to comfort Matthew but realised it was time for the twins to be together, just them. "One thing I do know is it's not the money and power that's important it's the love." Matthew asked "Do you love Daddy?" and Saskia responded hesitantly "Of course," Matthew wasn't sure how to respond. "All I know is that you're my brother and our mother is still our mother, and father is still our father, that's important."

After the initial shock and bad news, the last few days building up to Christmas were some of the best days they had. They went to view the lantern lights in Mousehole and joined the Sennen Cove village hall for a festive celebration. Rations had been implemented so food and drink that night was scarce and it was mainly filled with the women and children of the village. The school sang Christmas carols for a battalion of the British army who had come to build a lookout tower in Sennen Cove and be a watchful eye in this isolated part of England. Saskia was given a solo and Lowenna and Matthew were lucky that they were singing side by side. Then there was Christmas. Matthew and Saskia often felt sad about the turn of events but all this distraction was good for them.

Due to rations and a poor result in catches by Jim coming up to Christmas, food was scarce and Penelope was struggling to produce milk. Jim had been sick and missed two or three days of catches because he was in bed. Lowenna offered to go out, but they would not let her go out by herself. To top it all off, one of the chickens had died and the chickens were struggling to produce eggs, it was very cold that winter. The twins had always had Christmas in relative privilege, this year was different. Despite this, Jim and Mary wanted to put on a good show for their two beloved daughters and their young evacuees. On Christmas Eve, they received correspondence from Patrick for the first time since he ran away to say that he had been posted out to France as part of the resistance along the French coast and at the bottom of the letter wrote: *I miss you and my sisters very much. I think of dearest John often and he is with me every step of the day and is with you also. Please forgive me for running away, I will be home soon, Merry Christmas. Love P x.*

The children were downstairs putting up the stockings and Mary was upstairs crying. Jim came home late on Christmas Eve after a long day out on the sea bringing in a catch. He limped in looking tired but with a smile on his face and began by making jokes that Santa Claus wouldn't come if they didn't go to bed. "Where is your mum?" he said, curious as to why she wasn't in the kitchen or the living room. "She is upstairs," answered Lucy. He immediately went upstairs and embraced Mary from behind wrapping his arms around her. "What's up my dear?" he asked with concern. "It's Patrick…" she composed herself and wiped the tears away from her eyes. "He is in France." Jim looked at the letter and paused. "He will be home soon, he will get back safely, trust me." He kissed her on the back of her neck. "Come now dear, let's enjoy Christmas."

Christmas day arrived and for the twins to spend Christmas with another family was something they had never done in their life. Christmas in London was usually in their townhouse with mother and father with Charles' nasty parents coming to stay. Charles's brother, an Army officer, and his wife would visit. Betty would come at lunchtime and prepare the turkey for them. This year it was in a tiny cottage in the southernmost part of England. Lowenna sat out on the swing in the very early morning waiting for others to wake. It was at least minus 1 degree and the frost sat on the grass and swing. She was wearing a Santa hat she won at the village Christmas dance and contemplating how Patrick was and if John was looking down on them. That morning they all went to the local church and were greeted by the remaining families left in the village and they prayed for their loved ones out at war. After they returned home it was all celebrations and each child opened their stockings from Santa. The family couldn't afford much but each got a tangerine and knitted socks Mary had made. "Thank you," said Matthew "this is the best present ever," he continued as he looked at the socks. Meredith sent a package down which included two brand new coats for them and some extra ration cards for Jim & Mary she managed to purchase while she and Charles were still together. At lunch, Mary prepared a Christmas dinner the best she could. Food was limited but she managed to purchase half a turkey from the village butcher in exchange for her sending a Christmas card as a priority to the butcher's son who was on a naval ship up in the Hebrides. She had grown her own potatoes and veg, and Jim took some port out of the cupboard. Dinner was joyful and as usual, Jim was making jokes and singing Christmas songs. Homemade Christmas crackers were made by Lucy who was ever the creative one. Mary, throughout the meal, kept looking at Jim and could tell he was in pain.

"Let's go down to the beach!" yelled Lowenna after dinner. "Oh, I'm feeling a bit tired my love," said Jim "but go and enjoy it." Mary and Jim stayed put whilst the four children headed down the path to the beach. "Be careful it is still frosty and icy. I don't want to discover any of you have slipped off the cliff," he joked out the window as the pair watched them go. The four children went onto the beach together. Lowenna and Matthew held hands, looked at each other and smiled. "Christmas with you is fun," Matthew said sweetly and Lowenna kissed him on the cheek. Lucy and Saskia had walked ahead and were talking. The next thing had happened all rather suddenly. Saskia and Lucy stripped off their coats, shoes and socks and ran like the wind into the sea screaming, and giggling. Lowenna and Matthew looked at each other, laughed and followed in pursuit. It was so cold, but they just laughed and screamed like there were no troubles in the world. Jim and Mary could see them from the cottage and Jim laughed and Mary half broke a smile. "Mary, I have something to tell you," he said with hesitation. "What is it?" she replied concerned. "The cancer has spread," he responded immediately. Mary looked deep into his eyes, a small tear came out and she squeezed him tightly.

The truth is Jim had been diagnosed with cancer just after Patrick ran away. The doctor hadn't given him long, every day was a struggle, although continually and defiantly, he continued to work and bring in the catches. Mary watched in absolute despair each day as he had struggled up and down the coast path. The girls knew something was up with their dad but didn't want to ask or know the truth. They knew it was serious. He was determined to keep strong and defiantly wanted to believe that if he kept going, the cancer would disappear.

The children lasted about 2 seconds in the sea screaming, laughing and shivering at the sheer madness of what they had done. As Lucy and Saskia dived all the way in and the others followed, Matthew hesitated as his feet were covered by the ice-cold ocean, flashbacks of recent events rang present in his head. Lowenna ran in before briefly turning her head to see Matthew completely frozen in a state of shiver and panic. "It's okay," she reassured him and took his hand, "I won't let anything happen to you." They dived in and joined the other two. What a Christmas to remember thought the twins.

Jim and Mary lay on the sofa together, Percy sat in his basket wagging his tail, Mary stroking Jim's head as if they were the naïve sixteen-year-olds who fell in love all those years ago. "If the war isn't finished by the summer, I want you to always tell Patrick how much I love him," Jim said. "He knows already," Mary responded with reassurance. Christmas day was ending and it was getting dark. The children were freezing and ran up the coast path having dried themselves with their coats and socks, they were still dripping wet. It must have been almost below freezing by this time. Usually, Mary would have been very cross to have four ragamuffin children soaking wet with little clothes on invading their well-kept cottage but this time she did nothing. She smiled as they dried off and sat shivering by the fire. Jim looked on and laughed at what a crazy idea it was. The fireplace was stoking hot and they all sat around holding each other to warm one another. Later that evening Lowenna and Lucy sat on the sofa with their parents and hugged them. Saskia and Matthew continued to sit by the fire toasting their feet towards the fire. They didn't know this was Jim's last Christmas.

Chapter 6

In the days following Christmas, Jim took a turn for the worse. On Boxing Day, with the help of Lowenna, he managed to retrieve the lobster pots he had put out on Christmas Eve. Lowenna knew something wasn't right. It was bitterly cold, and Jim was wrapped up in every piece of clothing. Mary tried to stop him from going out, but Jim lost his temper. Jim never lost his temper so Mary knew she would have to let him. Jim had always had a sense of duty and stubbornness. As father and daughter, they sat on the boat with Percy sitting on the stern wagging his tail with no care in the world, Lowenna pulled the last lobster pot in. "Daddy, what's wrong?" she asked. "I mean you don't look well; your face is white and tired." Jim sighed "I'm not well darling," he responded, "you know after Patrick left, me and your mum went to the doctor… well they discovered I had cancer." Lowenna looked in shock. The weather was grey and cold and the waves much bigger than usual but for this moment time stopped. "But you will get better, won't you?" responded Lowenna. Jim looked down at the floor and paused briefly before looking up and shaking his head. "The doctor said there is nothing they can do for me, do me a favour Lowenna," Jim said. "Look after your mum, your sister, Matthew and Saskia whilst Patrick is away. That is an instruction." Tears began rolling out his eyes and Lowenna sat by him on the cramped fishing boat and kissed his daddy on the cheek "Of course I will," she said. Jim began to row but Lowenna quickly stopped him, "It's okay dad, I will do it, you need to save your strength." The pair moved positions and Jim sat exhausted, Percy sat beside him licking his face and sniffing the lobsters they had brought in.

After receiving that news, in the days that followed Lowenna grew distant from Matthew as they returned to school in January 1940. The cold winter nights were harsh and, just down the road, reports had come in of the enemy landing an aircraft at the airbase in Perranporth soon to be killed by the local army watch. By the second week of January, after Jim defying all odds, he could no longer muster the strength to work. His boat remained empty on the slipway, the village wondering why so few catches were being brought in. Other local fishermen became confused and curious as to where Jim was. Very quickly news spread around the village like wildfire and the family began receiving visits from the local priest, as well as receiving flowers and people coming to pray for him. By the end of January, Jim was bed bound and Mary cared for him round the clock. The children, desperate to help Mary as much as they could, started doing everything from housework to milking Penelope the goat. The twins hadn't heard from their mother since before Christmas and Saskia couldn't help reading the local papers Mary would bring home from the post office. The promise from Churchill that war would be over by the summer was slowly fading away. The Jago household was no longer the happy place the twins took refuge in.

On the 15th of February 1940, Jim passed away in his sleep his head peacefully laid on Mary's chest. That evening he had wished the children good night "See you in the morning," he said and kissed them each. But I think he knew this was the last time he would see them until they were reunited in heaven because as they left tears came out of his eyes. He had no strength left and the words he mustered to his children were incredibly hard for him. Lowenna came in that morning early whilst the others slept to see Mary contently stroking Jim's forehead. "Your father is out of pain now, he is sleeping," she said. "We will meet again." The last thing Mary said was "I love you" as he slowly drifted away. Lowenna came beside the bed and sat with Mary as she stared at her father. Lucy came in shortly after and wept like she had never done in her life. The twins sat together downstairs and cried.

The undertaker and the doctor turned up later that morning and took him away. That afternoon, the army, which had been deployed to put up the watchtower in Sennen, announced the beach would be closed off and began planting landmines on the beach. The Jago family and the twin's life had really been turned upside-down. In the days that followed, the village mourned Jim and the children didn't go to school. The funeral came and went and there was a very melancholic feeling throughout the village. A few weeks after the death of Jim, a letter arrived in the post from Charles to say the twins were to be shipped off to boarding school in India where they could be with their mother and be away from the ever-increasing tension in Europe. Mary mourned for weeks and grew distant from the children.

For a long time after the twins left Lucy and Saskia wrote each other letters with Lucy always adding onto the end of the letter "*Lowenna asks about Matthew, is he okay?*" and more often than not *"My daddy is looking down on us all, Mummy is not coping well without daddy but is growing stronger by the day."*

As the years went on and the war raged for another 5 years. Saskia struggled with depression, and at boarding school, she fell in love with her roommate - a girl named Susan. Susan's family discovered this soon after and removed her from the school. Along with her depression, it was something she couldn't live with and on the 13th of April 1944, she committed suicide leaving another gaping hole in Matthew's life. She had hung herself in her dormitory with no explanation apart from a small note written to Matthew. Matthew wrote to the Jago's announcing the death of Saskia. Lowenna read the letter and cried for days but never responded. She missed Matthew, her father, John and Patrick and had now lost another friend - she didn't know what to do.

In December of 1945 troops were coming home after a bloody six-year war. Patrick arrived at the front gate as Mary was hanging out washing on the line. Patrick looked at her and Mary looked at him. He ran towards her and hugged her. Mary cried in happiness and squeezed him like she would never let go. Lowenna and Lucy arrived later that day, having spent the day out at sea bringing in the catch, they hadn't seen their brother in six years. Mary wrote in her diary that it was the happiest day of her life.

Chapter 7

14 years later - June 1959 - Matthew sat on the steps of the Empire State building with his notepad in a black smart suit staring out into the distance. He had just finished 4 years working as a journalist for the New York Times and began working on his second novel. Before Saskia committed suicide, she had written him a note *Go to New York and follow your dreams – forever & always Saskia xx.* Lowenna had just landed her first plane in New York having flown her first aircraft across the Atlantic Ocean she was the only female British pilot at the time. The pair's lives would soon collide again, and they would eventually fall in love as grown adults. Their paths crossed in New York as if by fate.

Lucy sat in her art studio in St Ives painting. Patrick lived in Sennen with his French lover that he had met when hiding away in a French village with his regiment. He would become the most successful fisherman in Sennen. Mary was given full ownership of the post office in Sennen Cove.

With the very little money Jim had left Mary went on purchasing the post office after the previous postmistress took retirement. The post office continued to be the lifeline of the community. Patrick would come round with his wife each

Sunday for dinner. "Jim would be so proud of you", she would smile.

Mary would smile to herself knowing her three children were doing Jim proud every single day. She thought of the twins often and that Matthew would be coping okay without Saskia. One day, Mary hoped she would be reunited with Jim, John and Saskia. Until that day she lived with the knowledge that they would always be in her thoughts. Little did she know that Lowenna and Matthew would one day marry.

The Comedy of Love

The carriage tumbled along the road, the horses jerking it around and the driver on the top hitting the horses with his whip. Inside sat Lady Vester and her cavalier, George. In the distance, you could see the house of Lord Henry getting closer and closer every minute. The rain had stopped, and the bright yellow sun shone out from the clouds.

"I hope Uncle will be pleased to see us," said Lady Vester. "We have not seen him for a long time."

"Em! Well," said her husband. "Oh really darling, why do you take me down here? You know I don't like seeing relatives."

"Well, George, he's my uncle," laughed Lady Vester snootily. The carriage trotted into the yard at the front of the big house. Six big Labradors, two stupid rather jumpy Tibetan spaniels and two huge, scruffy wolf hounds ran to the carriage greeting the two people like never before. At the top of the steps, Lord Henry stood waiting for his niece and nephew in law to come up to him. The footman Edward took Lady Vester's hand from the carriage and helped her down. After that, Edward took the baggage to the top of the steps.

"Uncle!" cried Lady Vester. The Lord and Lady hugged each other, the dogs gathering around George. "Blow these rotten dogs," sobbed George. "And hello to you, my dear chap," greeted Lord Henry poshly. George just nodded his head.

"Well, you two, let's take you inside. James, take my guests to their rooms and then send them down to the dining room where I shall be waiting. Call the servants for a meal to be prepared."

"Very good, sir," replied James the butler. The footmen cleared the carriage off. "Good evening," said the footmen to the carriage driver as it tumbled off back down the road. The old butler, James, who was dressed in a black suit and wore white gloves, led Lady Vester and Edward to their room. "What a charming man he is," spoke Lady Vester. "Lord Henry? Charming? You're joking," mumbled George. "Who are you then?" Lady Vester spoke directly to James.

"I'm the old butler, my name is James but you can call me Jamie, my preferred name," answered James. The room he took them in was a huge room, with a huge bed, it had silken covers, with a dragon on them and velvet golden cushions. The windows had curtains that sparked with shining stars. When you went into the next room there was a bathroom. The first thing that you caught your eye was the bath. It was huge and had steps leading up to it, and on one side of it, there were three taps – cold, warm and hot. There was a mirror above the bath, and a set table on the furthest side where you could have coffee, "Well, I never," said George astonished. "This is brilliant, I think I'll have a bath."

"I think master wants you down for dinner," said James.

"Yes, of course," announced Lady Vester. George rolled his eyes.

"Well, I must be off to the kitchens," called James.

"Sorry to keep you," butted in Lady Vester again. "Yes madam," replied James.

"Is there any chance of our cases?" asked Lady Vester.

"Oh yes, Edward put them outside your door," responded James.

"Thank you," answered Lady Vester. James nodded,

"Well, I say, darling," laughed George. "I say, I say, I say." There was a pause and then a laugh. "I don't even know what to say."

The long, huge dining table was set, and the food was on the table. A servant opened the door and Lady Vester walked in wearing a turquoise, sparkling, twinkling, long dress with her hair done to perfection. She wore long gloves and bright sparkling shoes. George came in as well wearing a more boring and casual suit. He frowned at everyone. Lord Henry sat on his seat at the end of the table smiling in a condescending way.

"May I make a toast? This meal is dedicated to my dear niece and my brave nephew in law. May the feast begin," announced Lord Henry. The servants uncovered the first dish for them. "Why are you so rude?" mumbled Lady Vester quietly.

"I'm fed up with their ghastly arrangements. Bloody control yourself woman. We saw your father, Lord Francis, last week and you saw your cousin Jack yesterday, who owns so much land that he thinks he owns the whole world and now we are seeing your uncle."

Lord Henry looked up at them. Lady Vester looked up at him like nothing had happened. "How are you then darling?" asked Lord Henry.

"As usual," answered Lady Vester. "We've brought our ninth house in Surrey. And we've got a butler that comes with the house but the heating in our mansion is appalling. It's a rotter!"

"Of course, I paid for it," snapped George. "I've brought all nine houses out of my own money. You have not contributed to one of them."

The next day, George didn't speak to Lady Vester. In the morning he sat in his dressing-gown for breakfast sitting at the long table, his fists together.

"Your egg, sir," said James, holding a huge silver tray. "Coffee, tea, butter, toast also there on the tray." Suddenly Lord Henry walked in wearing his huge, long silver and gold dressing down.

"Do excuse me."

"Good morning, Lord Henry," addressed James. "Your breakfast is there as usual."

"Thank you, James," answered Lord Henry. "Morning, my brave George."

"Morning sir," sighed George.

"What's the matter old chap?" asked the lord.

"Argument… all night. I've had enough," shouted George,

"Oh come, boy, we're having a shooting party this morning. I suppose you've done shooting, of course?" pronounced Henry.

"No," answered George angrily.

"Well try it, you'll enjoy it," encouraged Henry.

"Very well sir," said George.

That morning there was a buzz of banging and blood. The wolfhounds and Labradors were enjoying themselves collecting pheasants, rabbits, and pigeons. Lady Vester was enjoying herself with the gun.

"Goodness my dear, you are an expert at this," complimented Lord Henry. "Why wouldn't I be?" laughed Vester.

"Come boy, it's your turn George," laughed Henry kindly.

"M..M...Mine," muttered George. "Yes. A...A...Alright." The old plump man picked up a gun from the gun rack.

"All you do is pull the trigger like that," demonstrated Henry as it went BANG!

"Eh! Yes, I think I've got it," he said scared at this point. He took the trigger, BANG! The gun's bang made him fall over.

"I'm a bloody fool," he said lying there in the mud.

"Oh dear," cried Lady Vester.

"Maid," called Lord Henry. Three maids come over and the footmen. "Yes, alright, alright, alright, we just need two. Go Edward, and you, Lucy, be off."

He was carried off to the house and put into the amazing bath. "Well at least it gets me out of that, and I can use this brilliant bath for the first time," laughed George.

The wonderful view from the window in the bathroom went down as the end of the day approached and the hunt finished. The poor rabbits, pheasants and pigeons that were shot were carried back.

The next day Lord Henry encouraged George to come for his cross-country ride. "Well old chap, all you need to remember is to hold the reins," reminded Lord Henry.

"Anyone would know that sir," said George like he was dumb. The maid helped him onto the horse. "Thank you, Lucy."

"That's fine sir," giggled Lucy.

"You are a charming girl aren't you," said George.

"Oh thank you," replied Lucy.

"Well I must be off," George said as he fell off his horse. "My horse is as mad as a, a, a,… as mad as Henry."

"I quite agree," said Lucy helping him back onto the horse.

"Bye…darling," said George as he galloped off. Three or four horses cantered over the grounds of the house being led by Henry on his huge black mare, slowly followed by Lady Vester. The horses galloped through the river that ran past the house. George fell off dramatically into the river!

"Oh blast," he shouted. That evening he didn't come for a meal. He sat in the bath drinking coffee and getting fed up. He had some music blaring out the room. He thought about what posh thing they might do tomorrow – punting, tennis, you name it. He kept saying "Oh God, Oh God."

That morning, he had been asked to take a boat trip and to do the punting. "Charming isn't it my dear chap," said Henry. "Em!", he mumbled, "I can't punt," losing his pole and almost falling in. "Eh, eh come someone help me?"

"Me? Course not, you can do it!" said the Lord as George fell in. "Oh my word, what shall we do?"

That lunchtime they had a picnic out in the gardens. George spent time drinking wine to get over all this 'rubbish'.

"Wine for you,?" asked Lucy.

"Who's that?" said George not knowing who it was. "Oh, it's you, my dear Lucy. My dear Lucy, no thank you, but would you like to meet me somewhere tonight and we can talk together?"

"I would sir, but the master doesn't allow us," the maid said softly.

"Oh stuff him, I've had it up to here with him," George complained showing signs of anger.

"Okay," agreed Lucy. "I will." As Lucy walked away George smiled to himself and thought, "Oh yes now we're talking."

That night he could not resist going for another bath.

"Oh George," snapped Vester. "You are always in that bath!"

"God, this household," shouted George.

"Do not insult my uncle's house," growled the lady.

That night, George sneaked out, and he met his dear beloved maid Lucy, who was in the library waiting. "Darling," called Lucy. Lady Vester was downstairs playing cards with his mad uncle.

"Lucy," said George. There was a pause. "Well what can I say, but how beautiful you look and what wonderful coloured eyes you have."

"Coloured eyes," sniggered Lucy. "You've got better-looking eyes than I have."

"Oh really," answered George. "I have had it with her and her mad uncle, but you darling, you are the prettiest girl I have come across in my life and… will you marry me?"

"Yes, why wouldn't I, but..." said the girl, then a pause.

"Yes but?" said George.

"What about sir and your Lady Vester?" asked Lucy.

"Sir, oh stuff them," laughed George.

"But, I'll lose my job… money," worried Lucy.

"There's no need to worry," said George. "I'll have it there for you." He thought and then came back to her, "We'll leave tomorrow, and in front of Vester and Henry. I think Vester can spend her time doing stupid things with her really stupid uncle."

"Yes, of course," replied Lucy.

That morning George packed his cases.

"What's this all about?" asked Lady Vester.

"I'm leaving", she responded.

"Leaving?" she said.

"Yes, leaving with the maid Lucy," he said. "My carriage is leaving at nine. I have informed Henry. And of course, once we have left, you and your uncle can be left to have all the fun in the world. Those houses can be yours. You see Lucy and I are leaving for India."

"India," said Lady Vester in shock. "India, you won't survive there.".."

"We're living with Maharaja in Bombay. The Maharaja is related to Lucy. Lucy is Indian."

"Well that's good, we won't have to put with your rotten rudeness," the lady said angrily.

There was a loud knock at the door.

"Come in," said George.

"Your carriage is set and ready," said James.

"Thank you, James, you've been a great help," thanked George. "But one last thing before I go."

"Yes sir," James replied.

"Give this picture to the mad lord to keep," asked George. "It's of India."

"Very good sir and thank you, sir," said James. That morning Lucy and James walked out hand in hand. The servants let them out. Lord Henry stood at the top of the steps with his dogs jumping around them barking at the couple.

"Well, old boy, all I can say is that you tried your best with all my activities, but you were rotten at all of them," said Henry.

"That's nice of you," George said. The dogs chased them to the carriage. Edward the footmen opened the door for them. "Thank you." Henry and Vester stood at the top of the steps watching on in disbelief.

"Shame, that pretty Lucy could have been my personal maid," said the lady.

"Okay sir," said Edward to the driver, "be off."

And the carriage rumbled back down the road off far away. And from then on Vester continued to visit her mad uncle, still doing the stupid things that they always did. George and Lucy lived far away with Lucy's uncle in India, where George created a bath shop with the Maharaja and Lucy set up her own silk company.

Veterinary Crisis

"Never mind," he said as the cat jumped from the chair and the dog ran through the door.

"Catch the dog, catch the cat... oh no! there goes the rabbit," screamed the receptionist. The vet in the green outfit ran out of the treatment room.

"Oh no!" he cried, "I was treating the dog." The other vet came out with a cigarette in his hand.

"Oh well!", sighed the other vet. "Makes a bit of a change."

The veterinarians turned quiet as the three staff looked at each other. Then 'slam', the dog-owning woman came out.

"What have you done with my little prince," she cried. She ran out and slammed the door, making the computer shatter and the noticeboard fall.

Then again, 'slam, bang, wallop,' the cat owner came out.

"The dog is chasing my cat," he said rushing out.

Coming out, the rabbit owner said, "... and that cat's chasing my rabbit!"

The waiting room went silent, except for the clock that carried on going 'tick, tock, tick, tock.'

THE END

Myth

A man stood by a woman,
He was a warrior of war.
A Viking who had sailed so far
And had floated to the shore.
He was sent to Norway, Denmark, and Scotland
And fought his way on the sands,
Until he sailed away from the kingdom
And fell far, far out of her hands.
He floated through the sky and space,
Shooting past aliens and all sorts asking
'Is this the human race?'
He was told to go to the underworlds
And was told live in dignity and peace
And there he would not be released.
He sought and wandered through the dead.
And asked himself "Is this the afterlife?" he said.

The Waves

The waves roll like an aggressive tiger
The big whitewash like a snowfall
The wind like a person whistling softly
The rain like a tear dripping from a person's eye
The thunder like an admiral bellowing to his men
The dark nights like a Black Panther ready to pounce

Moor Poem

All day it had rained on the moors
The rain spitting down on my hiker's tent door
The brown looking blanket that lay on the ground
The thunder and lightning that made a big sound
The wind and the rain that made the flaps quiver
The coldness and snow that made us shiver
The stove that made a rumbling sound
Warming up the atmosphere, which broke the ground
But then with a flashing magic and a change of weather
The place turned warm, and we walked together
Across the mountains, river and woods
Found a wonderful spot to rest- let's stop, we should
We stopped for lunch, drink and rest
We're walking that way to the south-west
So off to the west far and far
We'll walk, let us follow the guiding star
That settled over the mountain and lakes
The wonderful views made me shake
At last, we see some ruins of mining
A place where the sun is always shining
A place outdoors
A place for dining

Steeplejack

A steeplejack climbed up a church
Climbed high to mend the top
A man, perhaps a clerk
Watched him do the lot

The church clock went tick, tock, tick, tock
While the steeplejack with his hammer
Went knock, knock, knock

Then slowly at first,
Then faster and faster
The Steeplejack climbed down
Could this be a disaster?

"Well done," said the clerk
"Well done," said the preacher
"You're a hero the steeples are a wonderful feature"

Too many people who know me, this book will probably be the first time they find out I have written a book that has now been published for the public. *Some People Come in Pairs and other Musings* began during the first lockdown of 2020 whilst stuck in my flat in London and it was subsequently completed when I took a sabbatical and lived on the Isles of Scilly for 10 months whilst I was unable to perform throughout much of the Covid-19 pandemic. The inspiration of those islands helped me finish off what I had started many months earlier. During that first lockdown, my dance career had been taken away, like so many artists overnight. With my livelihood and creative outlet snatched away from me in 24 hours, I revisited my writing as my way of letting off steam, expressing oneself and getting stuck into fictional characters and stories I learned to really love. I have many people to thank, too many to name personally but to all my loved ones near and far – who have supported me over the years and seen me at my best and worse and supported me regardless, to *Austin Macauley Publishers* for taking a chance on my work and their countless hours helping to make this book half decent. And finally, to my year 6 primary school teacher Mrs Etherington all the years ago who said one day I should write a book and get it published. Not only did she encourage this but also to live all my dreams and saw the potential in everyone she taught. Since then, I have grown up and life has got in the way but 17 years later aged 27 here I am getting my first book published. The thought that if I don't do it now when would I ever do it? Life isn't about tomorrow, it's about the here and now.